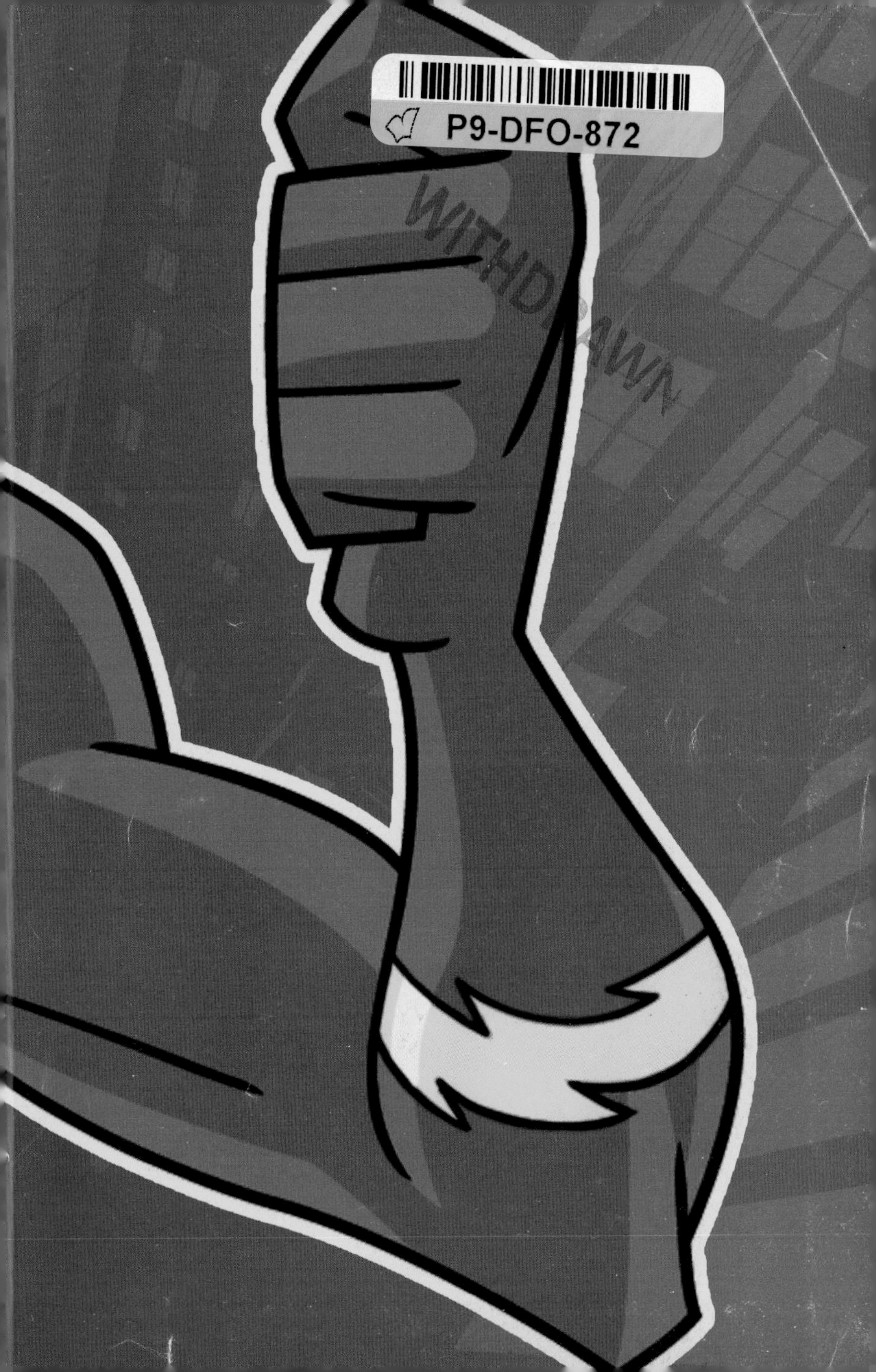

AFTER BEING STRUCK BY A BOLT OF LIGHTNING AND DOUSED WITH CHEMICALS, POLICE SCIENTIST BARRY ALLEN BECAME THE FASTEST MAN ON EARTH . . .

SUPER DC HEROES™

The FLASH™

WRITTEN BY
SCOTT SONNEBORN

ILLUSTRATED BY
DAN SCHOENING,
MIKE DeCARLO, AND
LEE LOUGHRIDGE

SHELL SHOCKER

STONE ARCH BOOKS
a capstone imprint

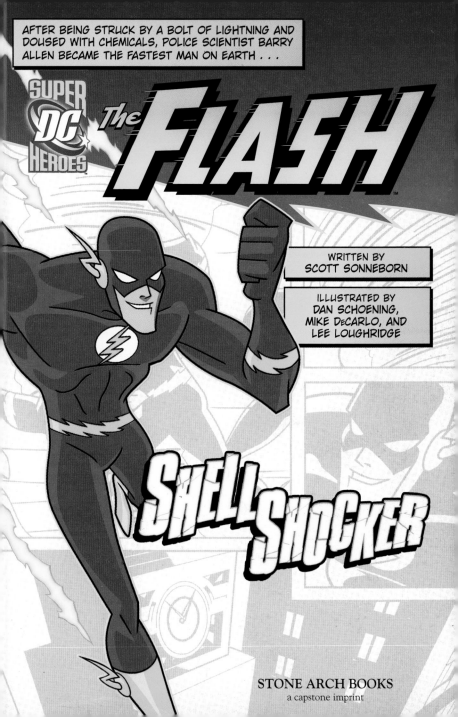

Published by Stone Arch Books in 2011
A Capstone Imprint
151 Good Counsel Drive, P.O. Box 669
Mankato, Minnesota 56002
www.capstonepub.com

Library of Congress Cataloging-in-Publication Data
Sonneborn, Scott.
  Shell shocker / written by Scott Sonneborn ; illustrated by Dan Schoening,
Mike DeCarlo, and Lee Loughridge.
      p. cm. -- (DC super heroes. The Flash)
  ISBN 978-1-4342-2615-0 (library binding) -- ISBN 978-1-4342-3092-8 (pbk.)
[1. Superheroes--Fiction.] I. Schoening, Dan, ill. II. De Carlo, Mike, ill. III.
Loughridge, Lee, ill. IV. Title.
  PZ7.S6982Sh 2011
  [Fic]--dc22   2010025350

Summary: Barry Allen has his hands full. While deactivating an explosive
for the bomb squad, the police scientist receives a call, tipping him off about
a robbery across town. Luckily, Barry is secretly the Fastest Man Alive . . .
the Flash! In an instant, he zooms out the door, stops the crime, and returns
before one second on the time bomb has ticked away. A moment later, the
Flash receives another tip, and then another, and another. Soon, the Speedster
suspects a link between the crimes, but even he'll be shocked when the villain is
finally revealed.

Art Director: Bob Lentz
Designer: Brann Garvey
Production Specialist: Michelle Biedscheid

Printed in the United States of America in Stevens Point, Wisconsin.
092010
005934WZS11

TABLE OF CONTENTS

CHAPTER 1

MOUNTAIN TOP

"Everybody, get out now!" cried Lieutenant Kistler over the police radio. "We are evacuating the station house!"

Everyone in the police station rushed outside. Everyone, that is, except Barry Allen. He sat in his chair in the police lab, staring at the bomb on his desk.

"Ten minutes to explosion," the electronic voice on the bomb calmly stated.

Barry was Central City's top police scientist.

Barry had a knack for solving problems quickly. That's why he volunteered to stay behind with the bomb while everyone else left the station. But this bomb was especially dangerous. It was designed to go off if it was moved even slightly.

"The Bomb Squad said they'd need hours to disarm a bomb like that one," squawked Lieutenant Kistler over the police radio on Barry's desk. Kistler was the highest-ranking police officer in the station. "What makes you think you can do it in less than ten minutes, Barry?"

"I can't really say, sir," replied Barry.

That was the truth. Barry was confident he could disarm the bomb quickly. Not just because he was a very good police scientist, but also because he was secretly the Flash, the Fastest Man Alive!

Of course, Barry couldn't tell Lieutenant Kistler that little fact. Having a secret identity meant there were a lot of things Barry couldn't tell anyone. That was probably why Kistler didn't like him.

"Typical!" muttered Kistler. "All right, you've got nine minutes to try to defuse that thing. That'll leave you a minute to get clear if you can't disarm it. Just promise me you'll leave the radio on. If something goes wrong, I want to hear about it immediately."

Barry was surprised. It sounded like Kistler was actually worried about him.

"That way," continued Kistler, "I can send someone in to clean up the mess."

Now *that* was more like the Lieutenant Kistler that Barry knew!

"Will do, sir," Barry said. He turned back to the bomb and carefully took off its metal casing. It looked like someone had dumped a bowl of spaghetti inside it. Hundreds of wires were tangled up with each other.

The key to disarming the bomb was to cut the right wires in the correct order. But with this many wires, there were a million different combinations that Barry could try. Only one would work. The other 999,999 would set off the deadly bomb.

Even the most powerful super-computer would take hours to puzzle through that many different combinations. Barry wasn't a super-computer, but he *was* a super hero!

Barry thought back to the night he got his powers. He had been working late in the police lab when a bolt of lightning crashed through a window.

The lightning had struck the chemicals in the lab Barry was working in. The super-charged chemicals splashed all over him. Ever since then, he had been able to move faster than the speed of sound. It wasn't just his feet that were fast, though. Every part of him got sped up by the accident — including his brain!

Barry got to work on the bomb. Thinking at incredible speed, he ran through all the possible combinations of wires. What would take a super-computer hours, he could do in minutes.

As Barry's mind raced, the radio on his desk buzzed with policemen talking to each other. Barry tried to tune them out so he could concentrate. But suddenly, the dispatcher's voice crackled through with an urgent update.

The superpowered criminal known as the Top was robbing a high-tech observatory on top of Mount Infantino.

"All officers on patrol are requested to report to the scene immediately!" shouted the dispatcher.

"Good luck with that!" one officer's static-filled voice replied over the intercom. "The road up to that mountaintop washed out last night! It'll take hours to climb up there. No one can get there 'immediately.'"

Barry knew the Flash was the only one who could get to the observatory in time to stop the Top. *Then again,* Barry thought, *I've kind of got my hands full.*

The bomb's voice timer called out, "Six minutes to explosion."

That isn't much time, thought Barry.

For the Fastest Man Alive, it would be more than enough time. He would catch the Top, and then get back in time to disarm the bomb.

In a matter of mere seconds, the Flash had put on his uniform and raced to the base of Mount Infantino. With the road out, the only way up was to climb. Even an expert mountaineer would need hours to make his way to the top. But in a split second, Flash had already climbed the mountainous peak!

On the summit was a small, high-tech building. *This must be the observatory,* thought the Flash as he raced through the door. He quickly darted into the building.

Inside, the hero found a giant telescope, dozens of futuristic machines, stacks of lab papers, and . . . the Top!

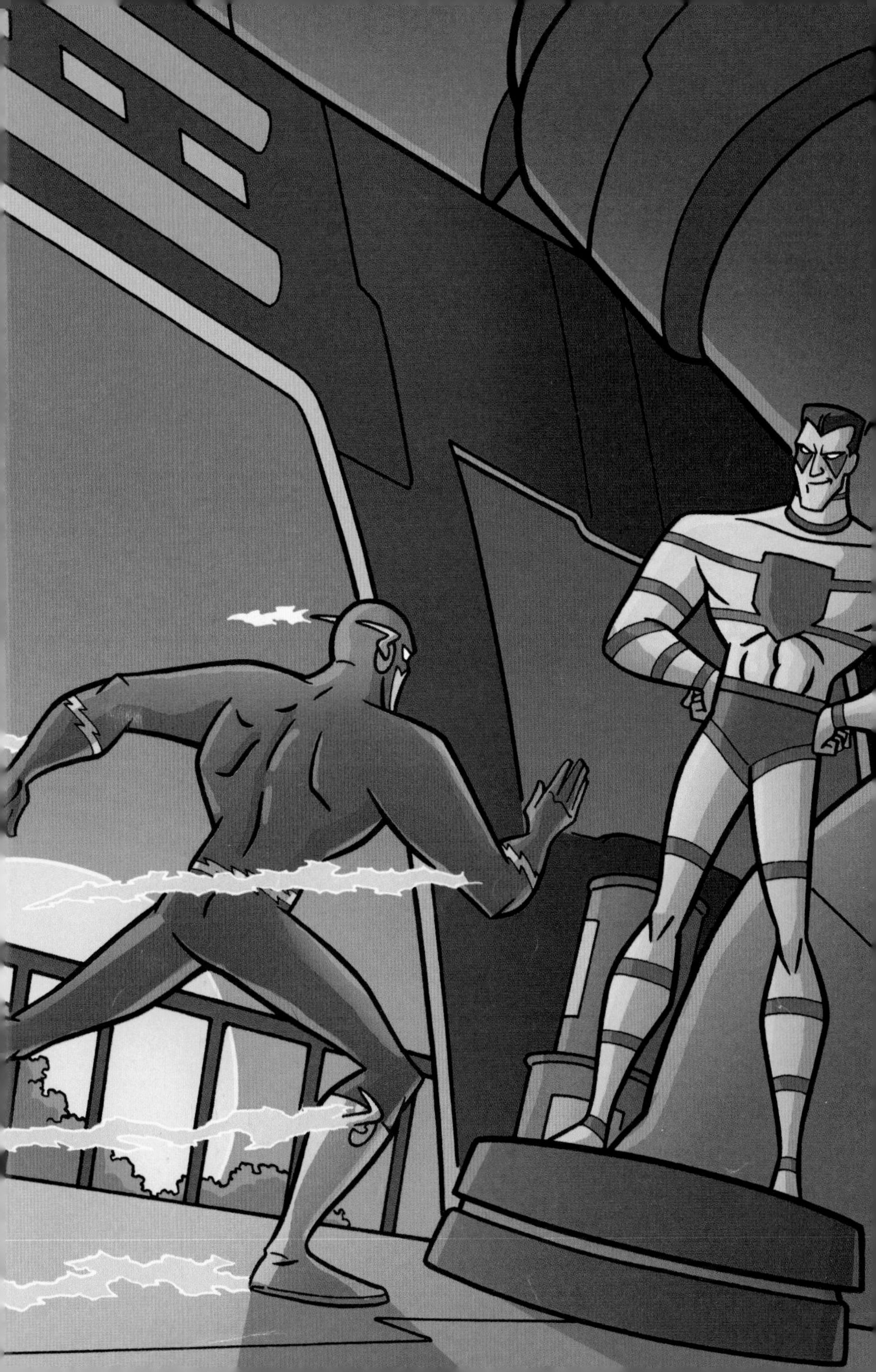

ZWWWWOOOOMMMM!

Papers flew everywhere as Flash rushed to grab the villain.

"Not so fast," said the Top, grinning.

WHOOOOSH! The Top started to spin. When he was spinning, the Top was almost as fast as the Flash. He spun around the lab, smashing everything in his path. Rotating at incredible speed, his body could slice through almost anything!

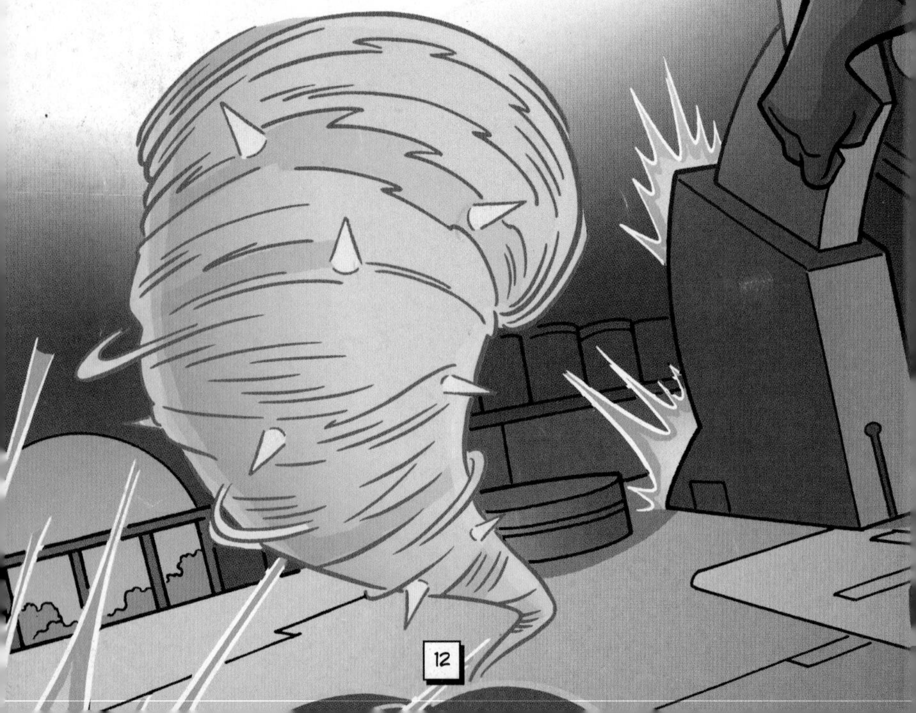

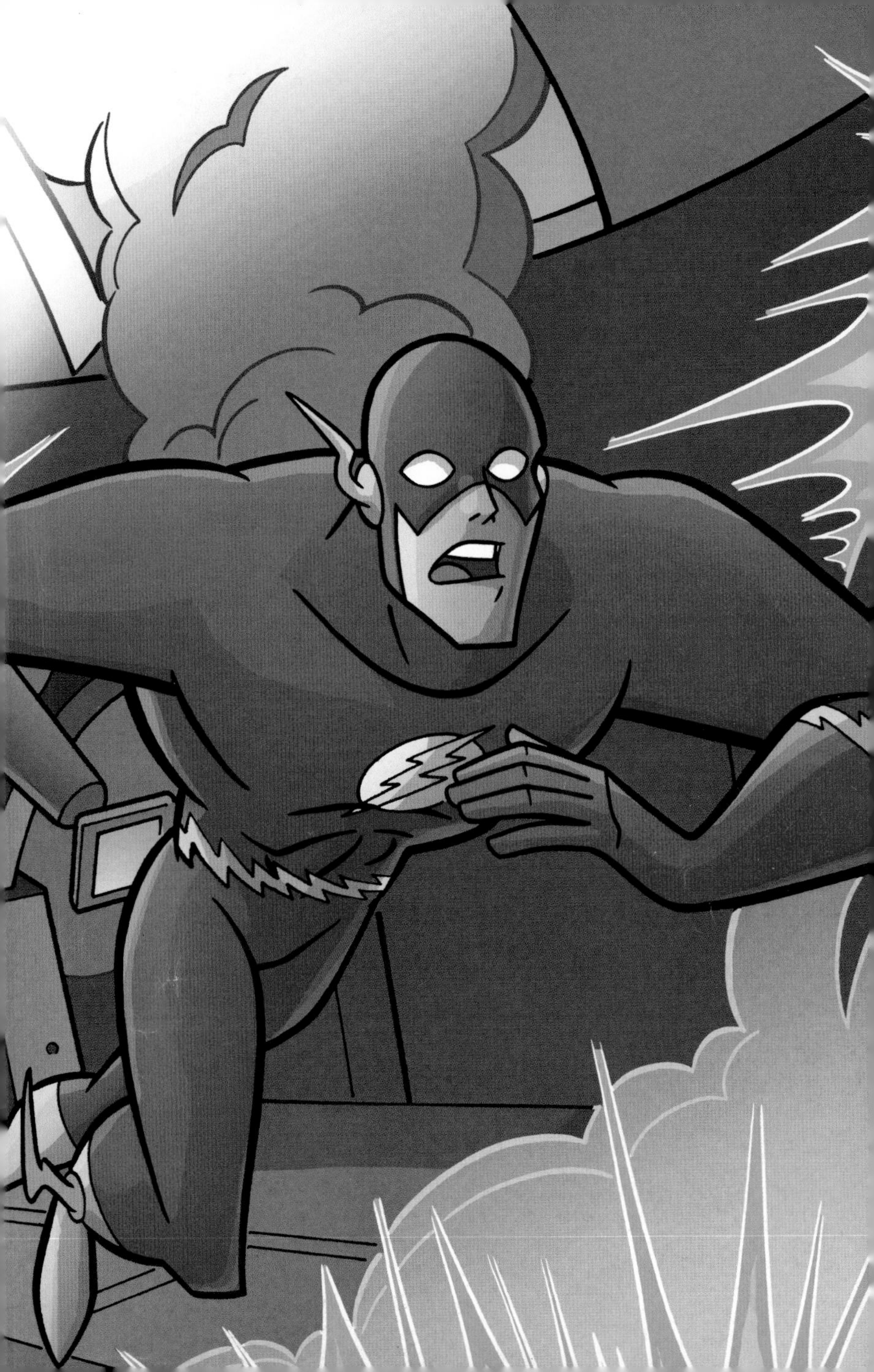

The Top spun right through a massive machine. **BaRROOOoOMM!**

It exploded into a million flaming pieces. Flash dived to the floor just as a huge chunk of melted metal flew past his head.

Smiling, the Top spun like a drill.

ZHHINNGG! He drilled through the floor. He kept on drilling into the rocky mountaintop.

Suddenly, a giant boulder on the mountaintop broke off! **CRAAAAACK!**

The observatory shook and crumbled. Part of it slid off the mountain and headed toward the ground, 2,000 feet below. In seconds, everything inside that part of the building would hit the ground and be smashed to pieces . . . including the Flash!

CHAPTER 2

TROUBLE ON THE LINE

The Flash fell. Huge chunks of the mountaintop and the lab tumbled through the air around him. Below him was the ground. It was a thousand feet down!

Slamming into the ground would be bad enough. Even worse, the rocks and the wreckage of the lab would land right on top of him.

The Flash's mind quickly raced through his options. *I can run faster than anyone,* thought Flash. *But I still need something to run on — I can't run on air!*

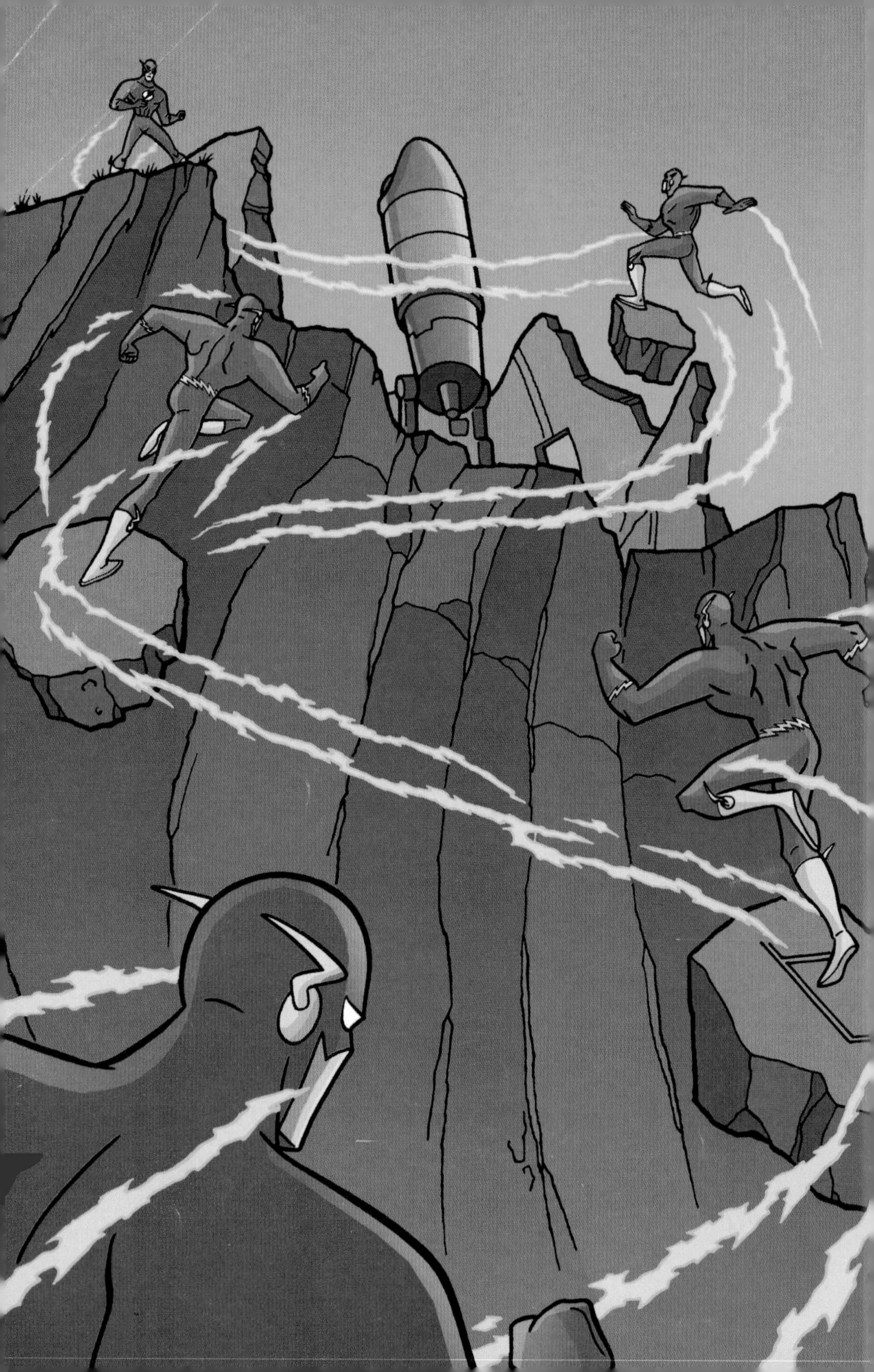

Flash looked around quickly. The only things within reach were the chunks of rock and bits of the lab that were falling through the air with him.

Moving faster than the speed of gravity, Flash ran up the falling rocks! He jumped from one to the next. As they dropped to the ground, he climbed higher and higher.

The rocks and debris from the lab fell all the way to the ground in seconds — which was plenty of time for Flash to use them to race back to the mountaintop. Back on the peak, Flash saw that part of the lab was still standing. He zipped back inside.

"Great," moaned the Top when he saw the Flash. "I was just about to call the newspaper and give them their headline for tomorrow: 'Top Stops Flash with MountainTOP!'"

The Flash didn't have time to trade dumb jokes with the crook. **WHAM!** Flash landed a solid punch. The Top spun around once and hit the ground. **THUD!**

Flash wrapped the villain up. Just as he was about to race back to the police station to disarm the bomb, Flash heard a voice. "Flash! Can you hear me? I need your help!" it said.

Flash turned toward the sound. It was coming from a pile of rubble. Was someone trapped in there?

His hands moved in a blur as Flash quickly dug through the rubble. He expected to find someone underneath it. Instead, he found a cell phone.

"Hurry, Flash!" the voice called out through the phone. The Flash picked it up.

"Who is this?" the super hero asked.

"There's no time to explain!" cried the caller. "Central City Dam is going to burst and flood the entire city. You only have ten seconds to stop it!"

* * *

WHOOOOSH! The Flash raced toward the dam at super-speed.

He had just a few minutes to get back to the lab before the bomb exploded. But it would take him only a second to see if there really was a problem with the dam.

The Flash skidded to a stop in front of the dam. It towered above him, a solid concrete wall 400 feet high. Behind it was enough water to flood the entire city.

Flash frowned. "What's going on?" he said. "There's nothing wrong with the —"

CRAAAAACK! Suddenly, the massive concrete dam shuddered and split down the middle! **SPLASH!** A thousand-foot-tall wave rushed toward him!

That much water will crush anything in its path! thought the Flash. Behind him was the Central City Zoo. All the animals inside were about to be buried under tons of water. Only the Flash could stop that from happening.

The hero ran straight at the water. He ran so fast, the friction from his boots turned the water into steam. Back and forth he ran. In seconds, all the water was gone, and the Flash was running inside a cloud.

The steam was so thick that Flash couldn't see. He was running blind at 2,000 miles per hour. **THWACK!** Flash's foot hit a rock, sending him flying.

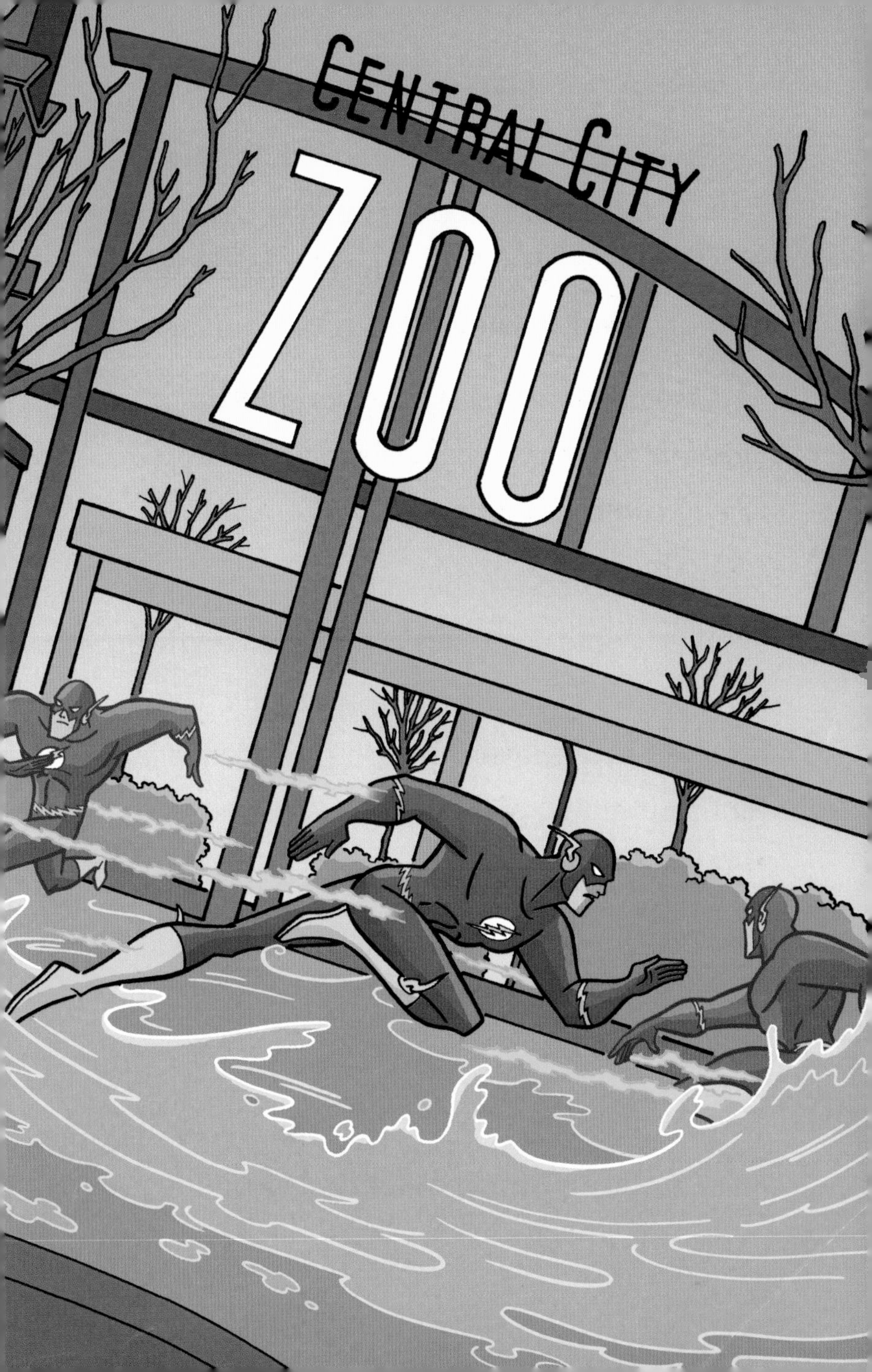
CENTRAL CITY
ZOO

The hero hit the ground hard, falling next to a jagged piece of concrete that had tumbled from the dam. An inch to the left and his head would have hit the concrete.

I should've known better, thought the Flash. *It's way too dangerous to use my speed when I can't see where I'm going.*

Flash waited for the steam to fade away. Soon he could see the zoo again. Everything was safe and dry: the lion sanctuary, the monkey house, even the old clock tower by the front gate.

Oh, no! thought the Flash in a panic. He saw the time on the clock tower. *I've got less than a minute to get back to the police lab and disarm the bomb!*

Seconds later, Barry Allen was out of his Flash uniform and back in the police lab.

Barry looked at the tangle of wires inside the bomb. Before he had left the lab, he had thought through 782,503 different combinations of wires to cut. None of them had been the right one. That left him 217,497 possible combinations to go.

The voice timer on the bomb called out, "Thirty seconds to explosion. 29. 28."

This is cutting it close, worried Barry. *It should be just enough time, though. As long as nothing interrupts me again!*

Just then, Lieutenant Kistler called in over the police radio. "Allen, have you left the building? Why haven't you responded?" barked the Lieutenant.

"Can't-talk-I-only-have-seconds-to-stop-the-bomb!" cried Barry in one gulp.

"What!?" cried Kistler in surprise.

Barry's face was suddenly as red as the Flash's uniform. Ever since the accident that gave him his powers, Barry's standard speed was the speed of sound. It took real effort to slow down so that he wasn't just a blur whizzing by. He had to concentrate to talk slowly enough for people to even understand him.

With his mind on the bomb, he had forgotten to do that just now. Barry had just talked to his boss at super-speed!

Barry was hoping he hadn't just given away his secret identity. Then suddenly, the cell phone he had found switched on. The caller's voice cried out, loud enough for Kistler to hear, "I need your help again, Flash!"

CHAPTER 3

OUT OF TIME

"Hello?" continued the caller. "Are you there, Fla —"

Before the caller could finish saying the name of his secret identity, Barry quickly stashed the phone under his desk so Lieutenant Kistler couldn't hear it.

"You . . . you," stammered Lieutenant Kistler over the radio.

"Sir, I can explain," Barry said into the radio. "I know the way I talked on that phone call must have sounded strange."

"What are you talking about?!" roared Kistler. "All I heard was the countdown on the bomb. You were supposed to leave the building if you couldn't disarm it!"

Barry should have been relieved that his secret identity was safe, but he had bigger problems. He had to stop the bomb!

Barry turned off the police radio and let his mind race faster than it ever had before. He sorted through dozens, then hundreds, then thousands of combinations. Red, blue, green, yellow — which wire to cut first?

The timer continued its countdown. Three seconds. Two seconds. Suddenly, Barry had it! His hands moved in a blur. He cut wire after wire. Red, then blue, then green, then yellow.

The bomb's timer clicked to zero.

And then . . . nothing happened. Barry had stopped the bomb!

But Barry didn't have time to celebrate. The mysterious caller was still on the phone. Barry picked it up. "Flash, listen to me!" cried the caller.

"No, you listen to me," replied Barry. "Who are you? And how did you know the dam was going to burst?"

"I can't tell you who I am, or even where I am," replied the caller. "The Top found out about my observatory — and look what happened!"

The caller paused, then added, "But that won't stop me from helping you prevent these terrible things from happening."

"What do you mean, 'these things'?" asked the Flash.

"That's what I was trying to tell you," said the caller. "There's another disaster happening right now!"

*   *   *

Flash raced though Central City. He zigged and zagged past parks and skyscrapers. The caller said that an abandoned building was collapsing — right next to a school!

Flash pulled to a stop on a corner. There was the empty office tower, right next to a school. Everything seemed normal, though.

Then suddenly, Flash heard it. **RUMMMMMMMMBLE!** The partially constructed building swayed and began to topple. The Flash raced past the school and around to the other side of the building.

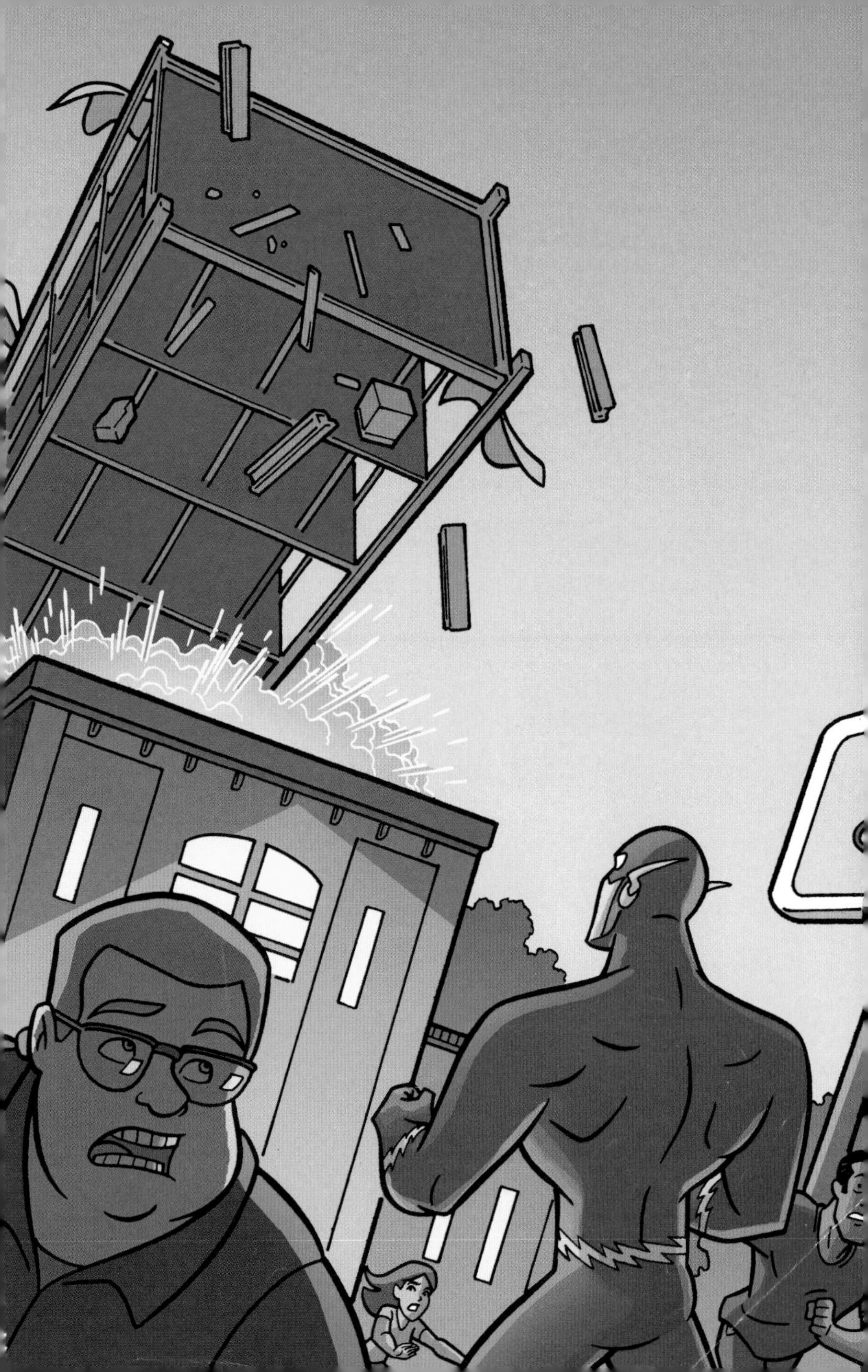

The school seemed safe for the moment, but several huge steel girders were about to fall on a grocery store. The girders weighed more than a thousand pounds. They would crush the store's roof and anyone inside.

How can I stop that? wondered the Flash.

The metal beams were moments away from smashing into the store. In a blur, Flash ran to one of them and punched it.

WHAM! The blow barely made a dent. But faster than the eye could see, Flash hit the giant girder again and again.

WHAM! WHAM! In less than a second, he delivered thousands of punches.

Quickly, he broke the massive girders into hundreds of tiny pieces. His punches turned the solid girders into a single, harmless pile of scrap! The store was safe.

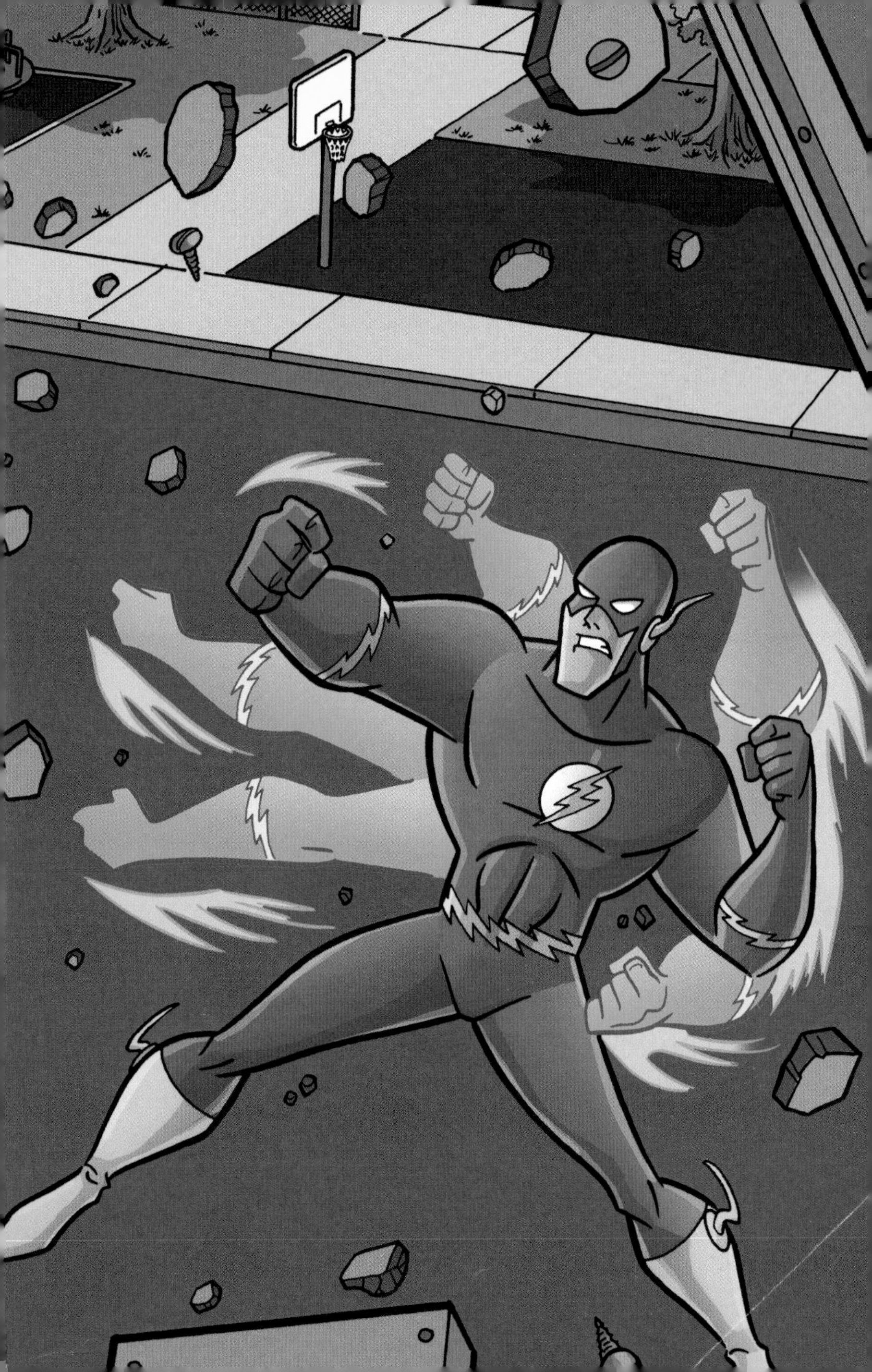

The shoppers rushed out and ran up to the Flash. A woman gave him a big hug. Several men shook his hand. "Thank you, Flash!" one of them said.

"I'm not the one you should be thanking," he replied. Once again, the caller's information had helped Flash save many lives.

I wish I knew who he was, so I could thank him in person, thought the Flash. *Then again, I know better than anyone that sometimes you can't tell people who you really are.*

Flash picked up the cell phone to thank the mysterious caller. Then Flash noticed something strange. The phone didn't have any buttons. There was no way to enter a number.

Something's not right, Flash thought.

There was a lot about this mysterious caller that Flash didn't know. Racing at super-speed, Flash's mind ran through all the questions he had.

How did the caller know about these disasters? Did he have the city under surveillance? Was he watching all of Central City?

No, because he couldn't have seen the abandoned building toppling or dam breaking. Both these things didn't even start until *after* Flash arrived. They hadn't happened yet when the man called him. Also, the caller said that if Flash didn't help, the abandoned building would fall on top of the school. However, when it started to tumble, it fell the other way.

Flash's train of thought was interrupted by the cell phone. BEEP! BEEP! BEEP!

The interruption didn't matter, though. Flash had already figured it out.

"There's only one way you could have known those disasters were going to happen," the Flash told the caller over the phone. "And that's because *you* caused them to happen!"

CHAPTER 4

THE TURTLE!

"You're right," said the caller. "I tipped off the Top about my lab. I knew once that crook found out about it, he would try to rob it. I caused the other disasters, too, with devices I had planted earlier."

"But why call and tell me they were going to happen?" asked the Flash. "You had to know I'd find a way to stop them."

"Of course," replied the caller. "I've studied you, Flash. I knew you couldn't turn down my calls for help. After all, how could you say you don't have time to help, when you're the Fastest Man Alive!"

"And as fast as you are, that's how slow I am," the caller continued. "That's why I call myself the Turtle! I knew if I wanted to commit one of my slow-speed crimes in Central City, I had to keep you busy."

The Turtle chuckled. "Of course, the only reason I'm telling you all this now is because it's too late for you to stop my crime," he said. "Here, listen to this."

The cell phone let out a squawk. It was followed by a burst of static. Then Flash heard a familiar voice. It was Lieutenant Kistler. Somehow, the Turtle had tuned the phone to the police radio!

Flash heard Lieutenant Kistler cry out, "All available officers, respond immediately to the First Bank of Central City. I don't know how, but the money in the vaults . . . it's all gone!"

The phone squawked again, and the Turtle was back on the line.

"No matter how fast you are," said the Turtle, "it's too late to stop me from stealing the money. Because I already did it!"

The Flash was surprised — and angry. It had been a long time since a crook had actually robbed a bank in Central City. Plenty had tried, but the Flash had always been fast enough to stop them.

"If you're as slow as you say, you can't have gotten far," said the Flash. "It won't take me long to find you."

"Well, that's not quite true," replied the Turtle. "First off, you don't have a clue where to look for me. You might know where to start, if you knew how to re-wire the untraceable cell phone you're holding."

Turtle snorted. "Only then could you use it to track me," he said. "But you're a super hero, not a scientist. You may think fast, Flash, but even *you* can't think through something you know nothing about."

"The second thing," continued the Turtle, "is that you're going to be far too busy to waste time looking for me."

"And why is that?" asked the Flash. His heart started pounding. He was afraid he already knew the answer.

"Because," said the Turtle coldly, "you're going to have your hands full trying to stop the biggest disaster ever to hit Central City! If you don't stop it in time, the entire city will be destroyed!"

HAHAHAHA!

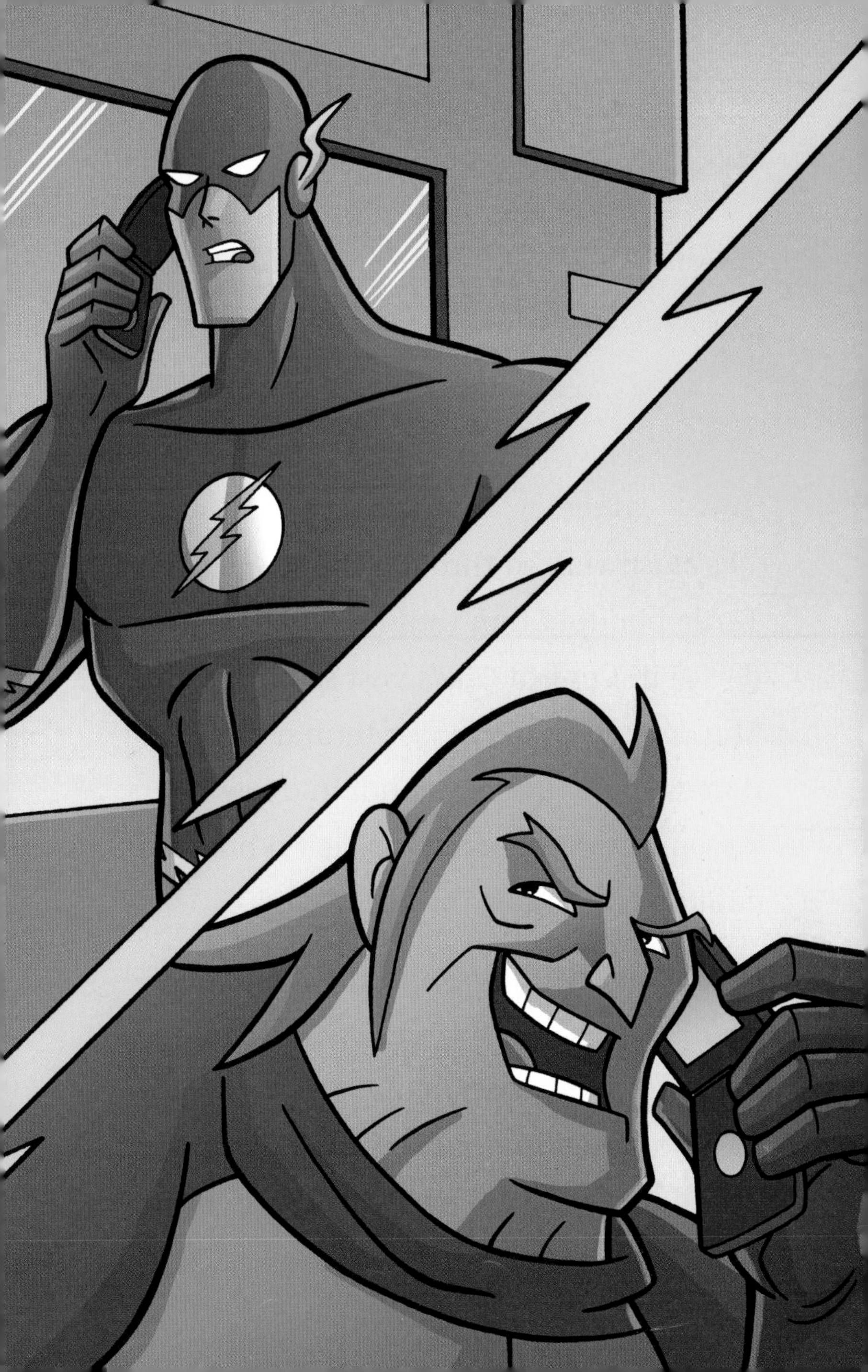

CHAPTER 5

SLOW AND STEADY

Flash walked through the sewers. The Turtle had told him that he had hidden a device in Central City's vast sewer system. The device was no bigger than a dime, but it grew hotter every second. In a few hours, it would be hot enough to melt a hole big enough to swallow the entire city!

Flash knew that finding something so small in the sewers would be like finding a needle in a haystack. But Flash also knew that he would find it eventually. He just hoped he would before the Turtle escaped.

The sewer pipes were like a maze. There were twists and turns everywhere. Some of the pipes were so small that Flash had to crawl through them. All of them were filled with slime, smelled like moldy cheese, and, worst of all, they were pitch dark.

If Flash ran at full speed, he could search through the entire sewer system in seconds. But there was no way Flash could move that fast here. Not in a slippery, pitch-dark labyrinth.

As Flash crawled through the dark pipes, he took his time.

I have to be patient, he told himself. *The Turtle may be a little slow, but he was right about one thing: sometimes, slow and steady does win the race!*

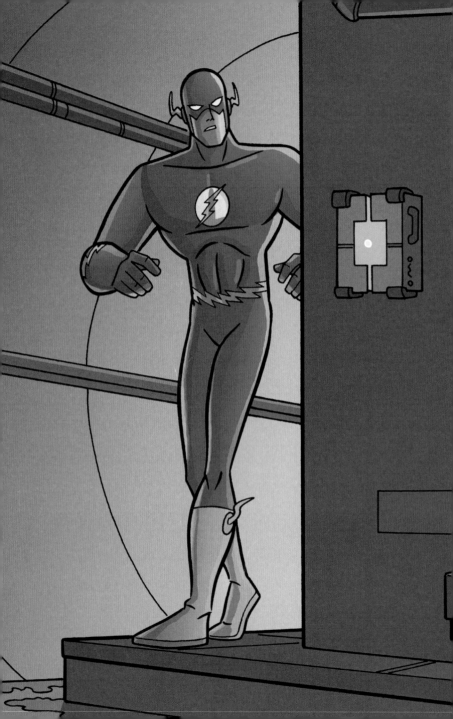

Above the sewers, a bus rolled along the highway. Sitting next to a window, a hunched man smiled. *There are faster ways to make a getaway than taking the bus,* the man said to himself, *but I like to take my time. I guess that's why they call me the Turtle!*

The Turtle looked back at Central City as it got smaller and smaller in the distance.

The city is still there, thought the Turtle. *The Flash must have found the device I left in the sewers.* The Turtle looked at his watch. *Still, it gave me a big head start. There's no way the Flash can find me now,* the villain gloated to himself.

He leaned back in his seat and patted the bag that sat in his lap. *It's amazing how much money you can fit in a small bag when it's all in $1,000 bills!* he thought as he chuckled out loud.

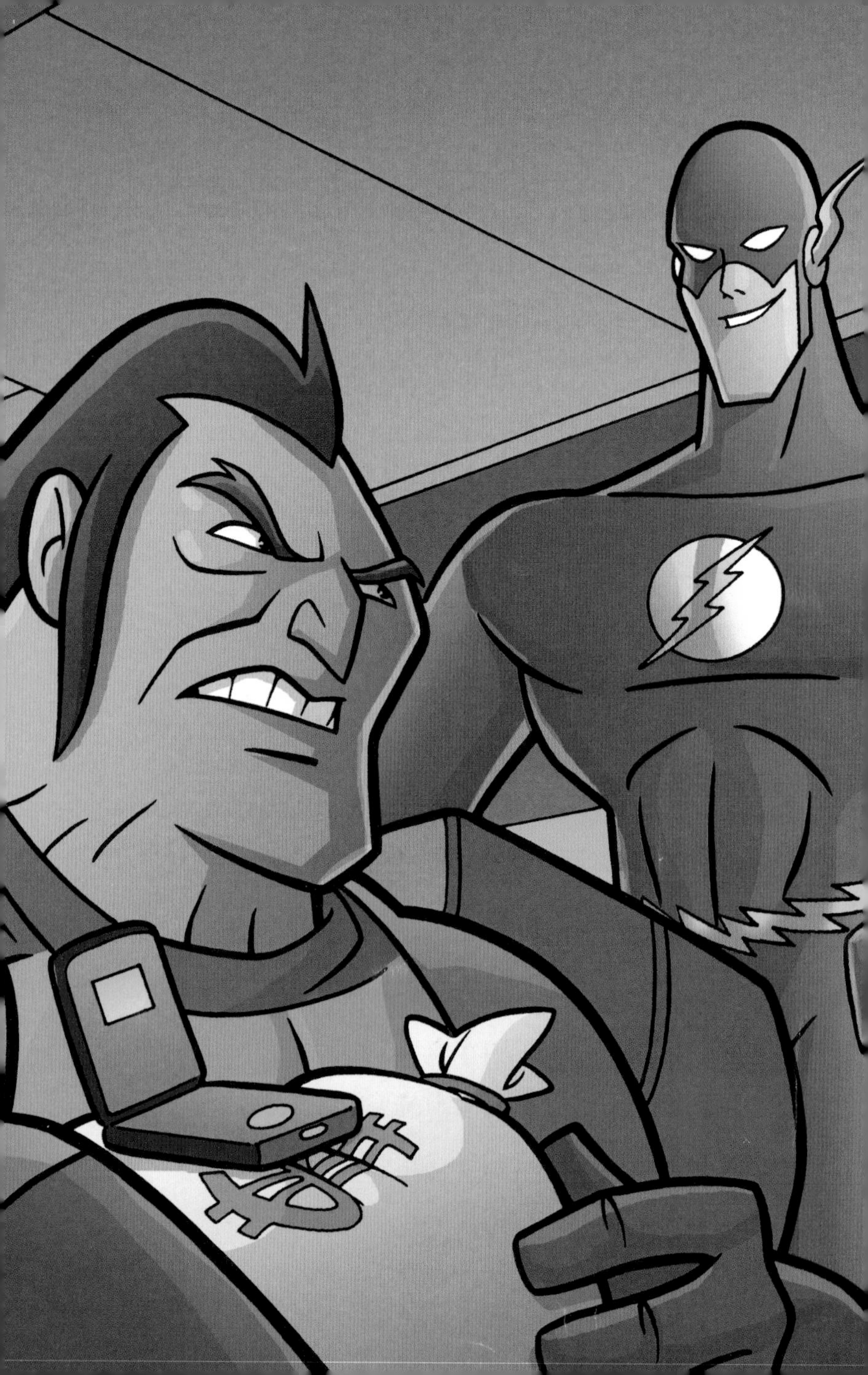

"Excuse me," said a man sitting behind the Turtle, "but I think this belongs to you." The man dropped something on top of the bag in the Turtle's lap.

It was the cell phone! Turtle turned around and saw that the man in the seat behind him was . . . the Flash!

"But . . . how?!" exclaimed the Turtle. "My plan should have worked! I studied you!"

It was true. The Turtle *did* know a lot about the Flash. But there was one thing about the Flash that the Turtle *didn't* know — he was also Barry Allen, Central City's top police scientist. As soon as the Turtle mentioned that only a scientist could figure out how to use the cell phone to track him, Flash had done just that. He opened up the phone and found a jumble of wires.

Just as he did with the bomb, the Flash thought through thousands of possible combinations to figure out the right wires to cross.

As a super hero, Flash moved at super-speed and was used to rushing around. But Barry Allen, Flash's alter ego, was a police officer. That job required a sharp mind and, more importantly, a whole lot of patience.

Of course, he didn't tell Turtle that. Flash didn't give him any answers. He just smiled, and said, "You're not the only one who understands the value of patience."

"Fine, keep your secrets!" snorted the Turtle. "I have one more of my own!"

The Turtle pressed a button hidden on his belt.

Instantly, a metallic shell formed around him. It was shaped like a giant walnut, and it was big enough to cover his entire body. As the shell extended around Turtle, it broke through the sides of the bus with a crunch! Inside his protective shell, the Turtle was now sandwiched between the interior walls of the vehicle.

Flash evacuated the bus driver and all the passengers. Once he was certain that everyone was safe, he plopped down in the driver's seat.

"Neat trick," Flash admitted.

"It's no trick, Flash!" Turtle howled from inside his defensive shield. "My shell is too strong to break through, and I've designed it so that your super-speed powers can't move it! You're not getting me out of here until I decide to come out!"

"That's okay," replied the Flash. "I'm in no rush." He turned the key and started the bus's engine. Flash smiled as he shifted the bus into gear. VROOOOOOM!

"Wha — what's going on?!" Turtle said.

Slowly but surely, the bus lurched forward. Flash drove down the city street — with the shell-shocked villain in tow.

Flash grinned. "I've been rushing around town all day, thanks to you," he said. "So I think we'll go on a nice, leisurely ride together — to Central City Prison!"

Maybe this bus wasn't the best plan after all, thought Turtle. *Next time, I'm taking a cab!*

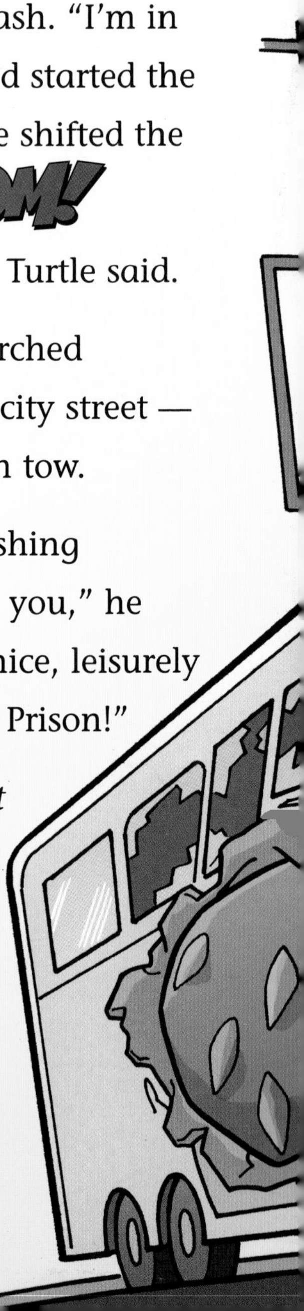

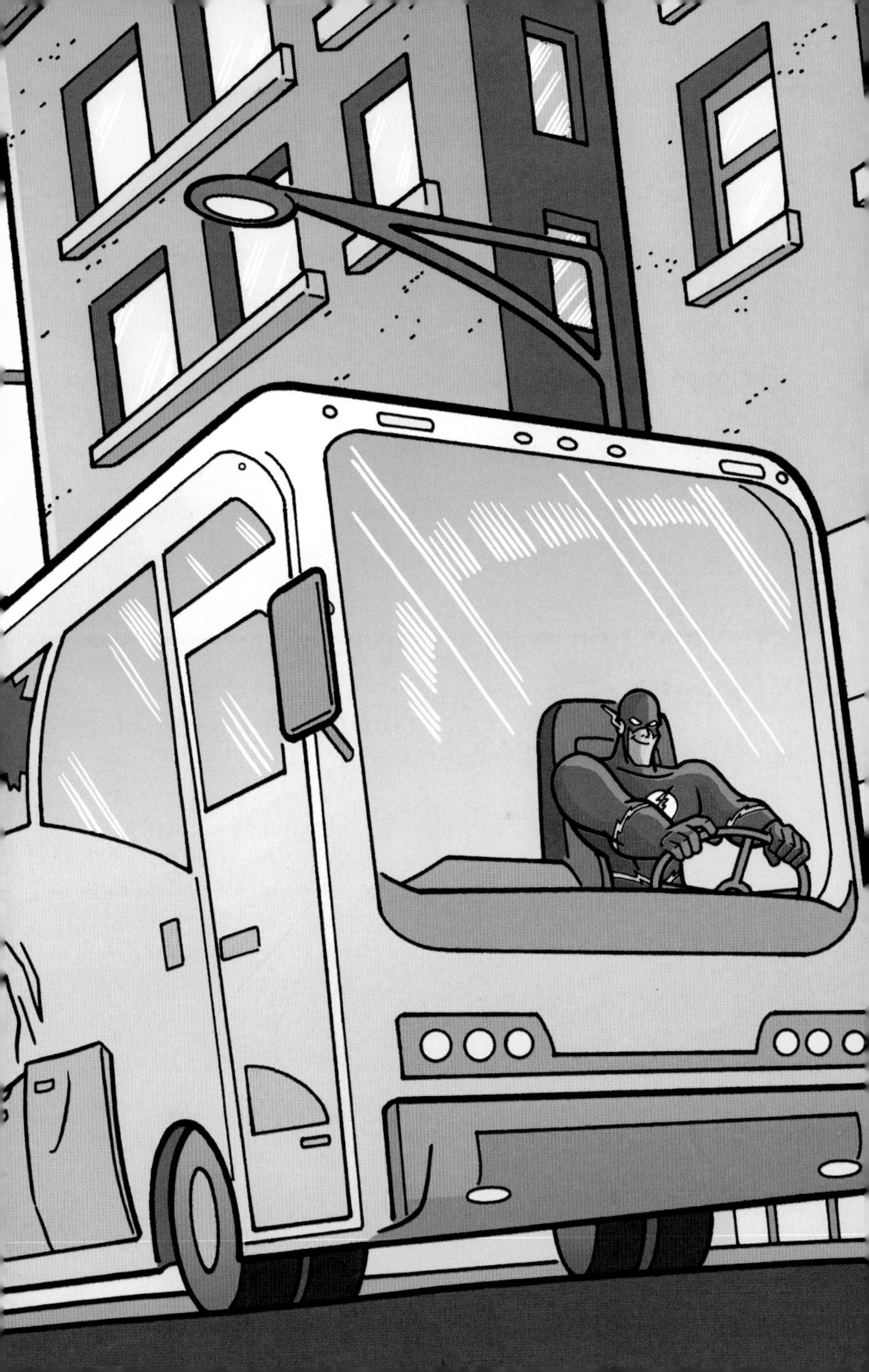

File Edit View Go Window Help

TURTLE

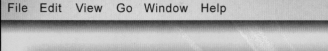

THE TURTLE

REAL NAME: UNKNOWN

OCCUPATION: CRIMINAL MASTERMIND

HEIGHT: 5' 2"

WEIGHT: 357 LBS.

EYES: BLACK

HAIR: GRAY

SPECIAL POWERS/ABILITIES:

Super-slowness; unmatched planning and organizational techniques allow for clever crimes; indestructible turtle shell; longevity; thick skin, both physically and mentally.

done

Tue 6:23:12 PM Barry Allen

TURTLE BIO

BIOGRAPHY:

Growing up, young Turtle had a tough time keeping up with his fast-paced friends. At first, his slowness turned to shyness. However, this slow-motion super-villain soon came out of his shell, turning to a life of crime. As a criminal mastermind in Central City, the Turtle uses slowness to his advantage. Although his clever crimes take plenty of time, they are often very effective. With a super-strong shell and extra long life span, the Flash could be chasing this reptile robber for years to come.

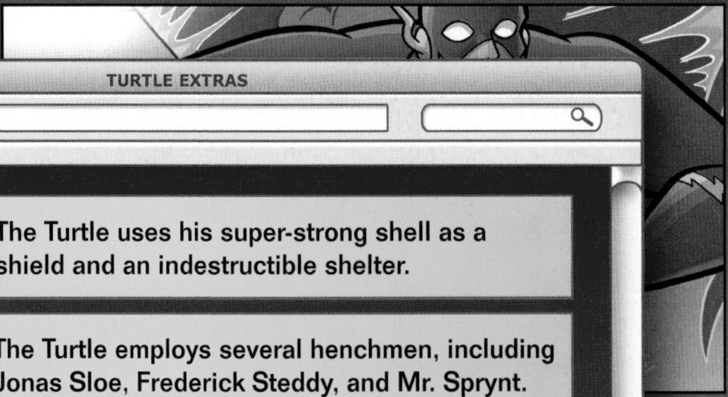

TURTLE EXTRAS

The Turtle uses his super-strong shell as a shield and an indestructible shelter.

The Turtle employs several henchmen, including Jonas Sloe, Frederick Steddy, and Mr. Sprynt.

The Turtle says, "Slow and steady wins the race!" He'll do anything to prove that he's right.

BIOGRAPHIES

Scott Sonneborn has written 20 books, one circus (for Ringling Bros. Barnum & Bailey), and a bunch of TV shows. He's been nominated for one Emmy and spent three very cool years working at DC Comics. He lives in Los Angeles with his wife and their two sons.

Dan Schoening was born in Victoria, B.C., Canada. From an early age, Dan has had a passion for animation and comic books. Currently, Dan does freelance work in the animation and game industry and spends a lot of time with his lovely little daughter, Paige.

Mike DeCarlo is a longtime contributor of comic art whose range extends from Batman and Iron Man to Bugs Bunny and Scooby-Doo. He resides in Connecticut with his wife and four children.

Lee Loughridge has been working in comics for more than fifteen years. He currently lives in sunny California in a tent on the beach.

GLOSSARY

abandoned (uh-BAN-duhnd)—deserted, or no longer in use

defuse (dee-FYOOZ)—to remove the fuse, or stop a bomb from exploding

girder (GUR-dur)—a large, heavy beam made of steel or concrete that is used in construction

intercom (IN-tur-kom)—a speaker system that allows someone to listen and talk to a person in another room

labyrinth (LA-buh-renth)—a complex maze

observatory (uhb-ZUR-vuh-tor-ee)—a building containing telescopes and other instruments for studying the sky and the stars

sanctuary (SANGK-choo-er-ee)—an area where animals are protected

summit (SUHM-it)—the highest point of a mountain

urgent (UR-juhnt)—something that needs quick or immediate attention

DISCUSSION QUESTIONS

1. The Turtle plans his attacks very carefully. The Flash takes immediate action. Which type of person are you? Do you plan things out or act quickly?

2. How do you think the Turtle should be punished for his crimes? Explain your answer.

3. Flash's superpower is super-speed. If you could choose one superpower, what would it be? Why?

WRITING PROMPTS

1. Flash faces off against many different villains. Come up with your own enemy of the Scarlet Speedster. What would your villain look like? What's your villain's name?

2. Write about a time that you used speed to save the day. Did you make a running catch in baseball? Did you sprint to stop a crime? Write about your speedy experience.

3. Imagine you could run as fast as the Flash. Where would you go? What places would you see? Write about having super-speed for a day!

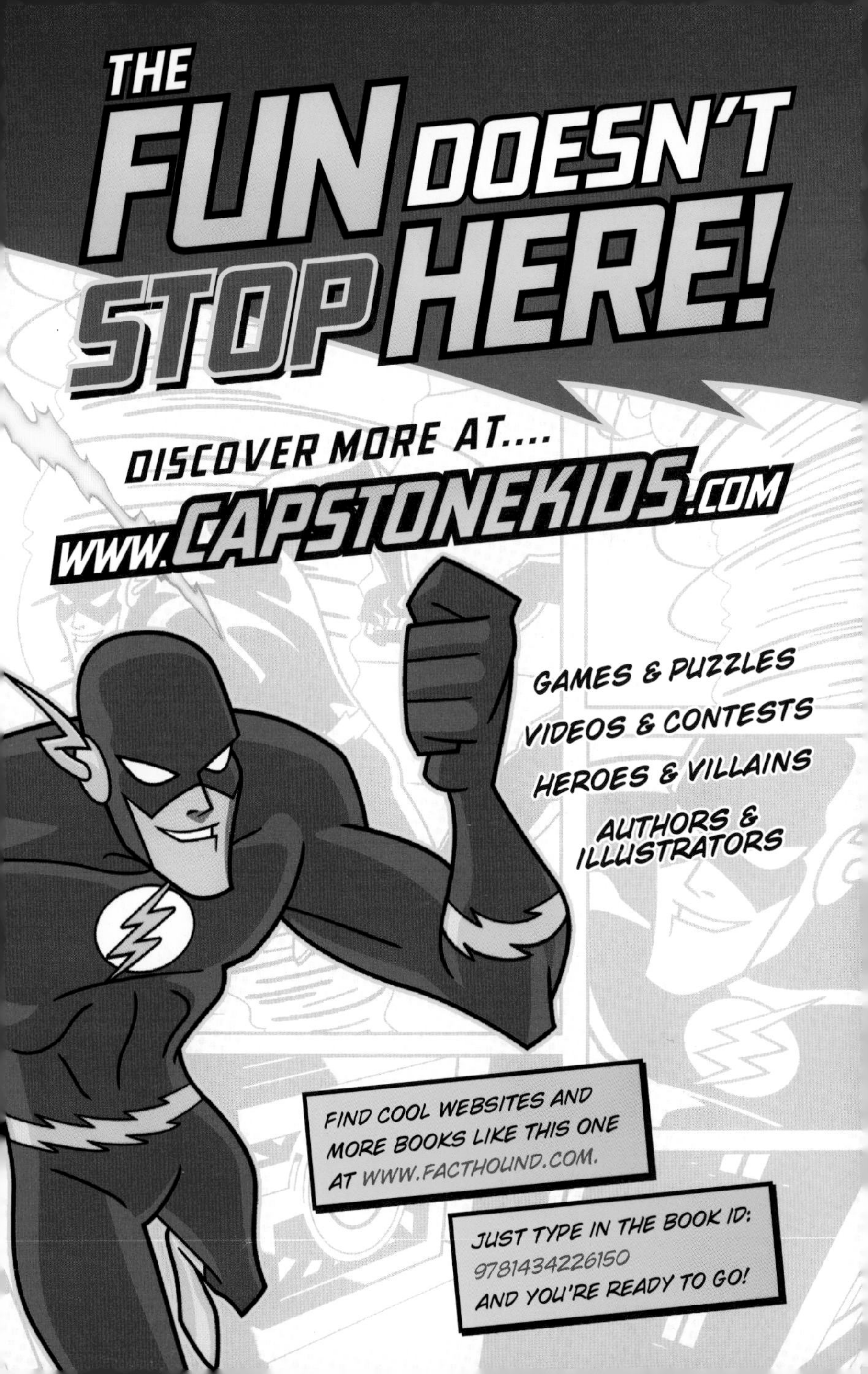
THE FUN DOESN'T STOP HERE!
DISCOVER MORE AT....
WWW.CAPSTONEKIDS.COM
GAMES & PUZZLES
VIDEOS & CONTESTS
HEROES & VILLAINS
AUTHORS & ILLUSTRATORS
FIND COOL WEBSITES AND MORE BOOKS LIKE THIS ONE AT WWW.FACTHOUND.COM.
JUST TYPE IN THE BOOK ID: 9781434226150 AND YOU'RE READY TO GO!

MORE NEW *The* FLASH ADVENTURES!

SUPER DC HEROES
The FLASH
LEMKE
DOESCHER
DICARLO
LOUGHRIDGE
WRATH OF THE WEATHER WIZARD

WRATH OF THE WEATHER WIZARD

SUPER DC HEROES
The FLASH
ATTACK OF PROFESSOR ZOOM!

ATTACK OF PROFESSOR ZOOM!

SUPER DC HEROES
The FLASH
SHADOW OF THE SUN

SHADOW OF THE SUN

SUPER DC HEROES
The FLASH
CAPTAIN COLD'S ARCTIC ERUPTION

CAPTAIN COLD'S ARCTIC ERUPTION

SUPER DC HEROES
The FLASH
GORILLA WARFARE

GORILLA WARFARE

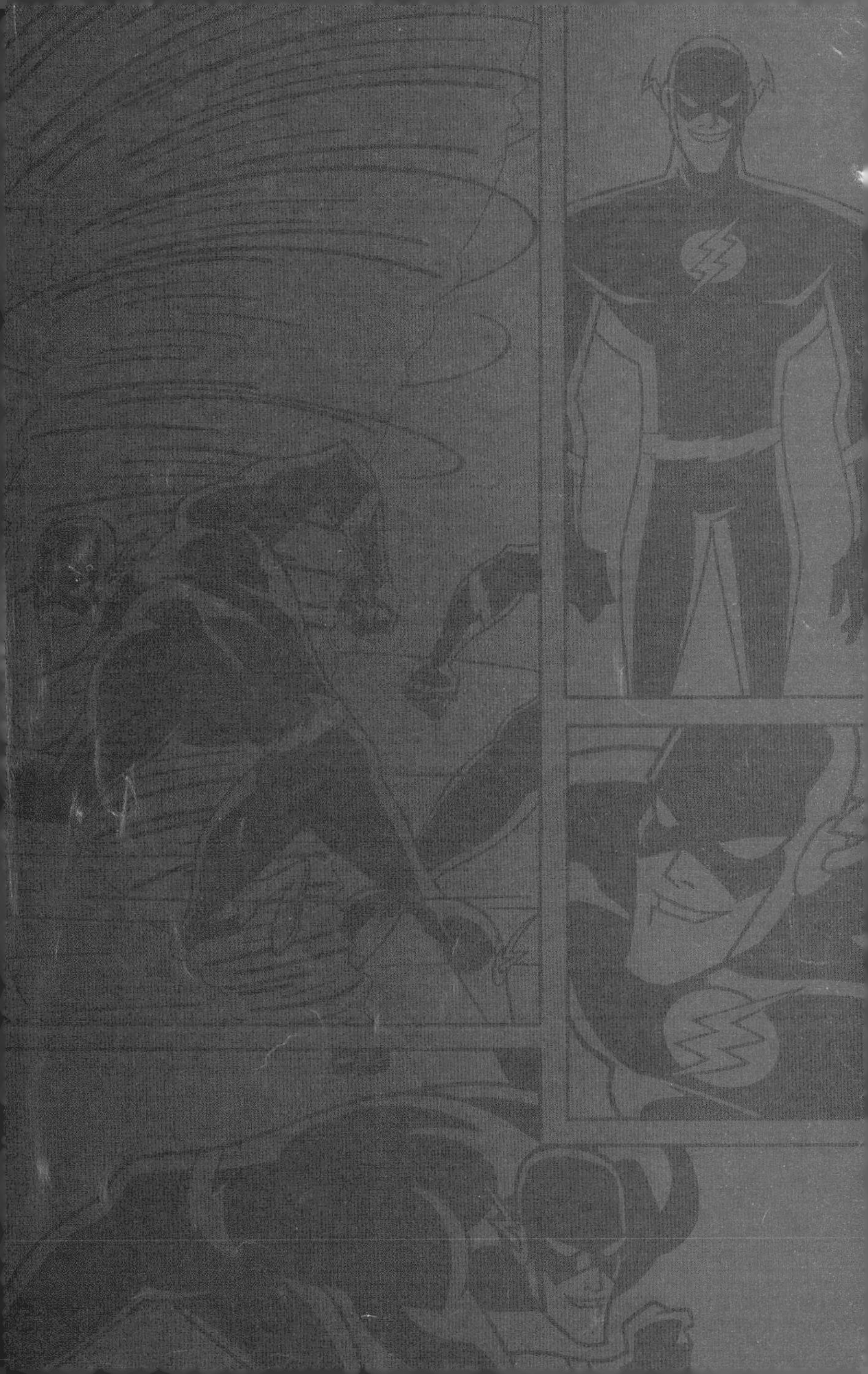

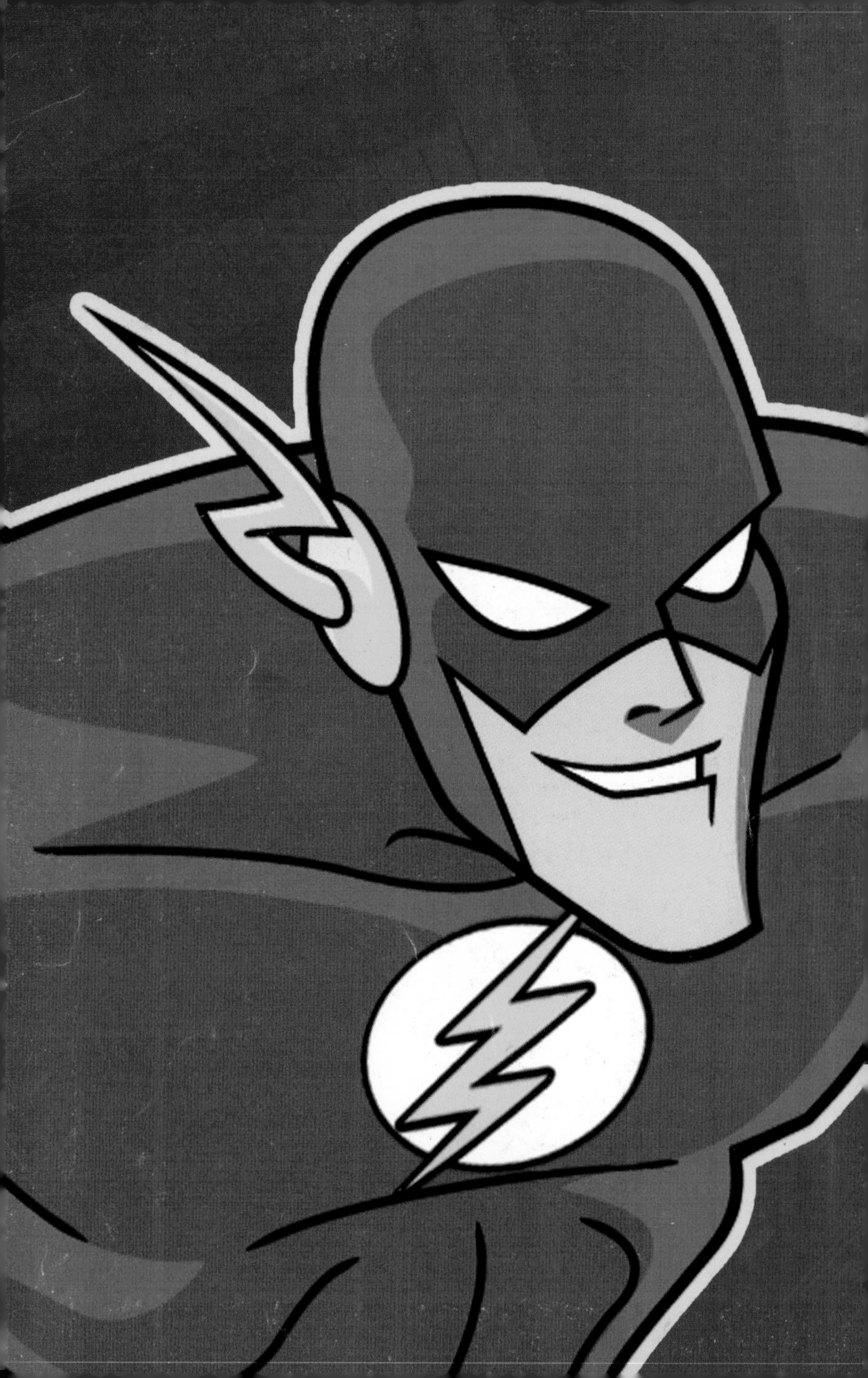